For Clara, again, with love

1 3 5 7 9 10 8 6 4 2

Copyright © Shirley Hughes 1998

Shirley Hughes has asserted her right under the Copyright,
Designs and Patents Act, 1988, to be identified as the author
and illustrator of this work

First published in the United Kingdom 1998
by The Bodley Head Children's Books
Random House, 20 Vauxhall Bridge Road, London SW1V 2SA

Random House Australia (Pty) Limited
20 Alfred Street, Milsons Point, Sydney
New South Wales 2061, Australia

Random House New Zealand Limited
18 Poland Road, Glenfield
Auckland 10, New Zealand

Random House South Africa (Pty) Limited
Endulini, 5A Jubilee Road,
Parktown 2193, South Africa

Random House UK Limited Reg. No. 954009

A CIP catalogue record for this book
is available from the British Library

ISBN 0 370 32475 7

Printed in Singapore

THE
LION AND THE
UNICORN

Shirley Hughes

THE BODLEY HEAD
LONDON

'LONDON'S burning,
London's burning!
Fetch the engines,
fetch the engines!
Fire, fire! Fire, fire!
Pour on water,
pour on water!'

Every evening, soon after
dark, the warning sirens
wailed. Then came the
awful droning of enemy
aircraft overhead, and fire-
bombs and explosives
whined and whistled out
of the sky.

LENNY Levi and his mum huddled together under the stairs. Lenny clutched the badge that his dad had given him before he went away. It was made of solid brass; a lion and a unicorn up on their hind legs, fighting each other. Lenny kept it in his pocket always where he could feel it.

Dad was fighting too. He was in the army far away while Lenny and Mum clung to one another and longed for daylight.

A unicorn was a mythical beast, Dad had told him. A mysterious, gentle creature. But lions were real, all right.

LIONS stood for being brave. Everybody had to be brave in wartime, not only soldiers but other people too. Children even. 'Be a brave boy, Lenny,' Dad had told him when they said goodbye.

Sometimes they got letters from Dad. They came in batches, two or three at a time. Those were the best days. Mum read bits out to Lenny while he was having his tea. Dad always put in a drawing for him. Sometimes it was a funny picture like the one of the Sergeant. Once he did a beautiful picture of a unicorn with flowers around its neck.

ONE night the bangs shook the house so badly that they thought the roof would fall in. 'We should have gone to the shelter,' muttered Mum.

Next morning, when they went out, the Robinsons' house wasn't there any more. Their things were lying all over the street amongst the rubble and broken glass. The neighbours said that the Robinsons had gone to the Rest Centre in the night, wearing blankets.

'That's it!' said Mum. 'We've got to get you out of here, Lenny.'

Soon, suitcase packed and his name on a label pinned to his jacket, clutching his precious badge in his pocket, Lenny joined a crowd of other children at the railway station. Mum was there to see him off.

Lenny felt the shape of the lion with his fingertips. He knew he was supposed to be brave. But when he saw so many strange faces he didn't know how to be.

'It'll be a lovely place in the country,' Mum told him. 'Flowers and rabbits and that.' But she was nearly crying.

LENNY only realised what was really happening when he was in a crowded railway carriage. He put his head out of the window and shouted: 'Don't leave me, Mum! You come with me!'

But the train had already started to move, very slowly at first, then fast gaining speed. 'I'll come to see you soon!' called Mum. 'Be a good boy.' She was a white face amongst all the others. She shouted something else but Lenny couldn't hear her. Then she was a tiny figure at the end of the platform, waving and waving.

IT was so dark when at last
Lenny arrived that he could
not see the place. The
windows were blacked out.
Then all at once he was in a
huge hall, so big that it
seemed their whole house in
London could have fitted
into it easily.

There were no rabbits that
Lenny could see. Just some
tired grownups bustling
about, and two girls bigger
than him who were called
Joyce and Patsy, with a little
one called Winnie. They
were evacuees. Lenny was
one too.

A lady wearing a great
many scarves and woolly
cardigans said: 'I am Lady
De Vass. You must be very
tired. Nanny will give you
your supper and show you
where you are going to
sleep.'

'We specially asked for girls,'
Nanny complained, eyeing
Lenny.

'I'm afraid it's too late now,
Nanny,' said Lady De Vass.
'And he is not a very big
boy,' she added kindly.

THE evacuees were to
sleep in a big attic room with
dark beams overhead. It was
chilly and had no electric
light or carpets but there was
a nice woody smell. A
curtain hung down the
middle. Joyce, Patsy and
Winnie were together on one
side and Lenny was alone on
the other.

NANNY left a couple of
little lamps burning when
she said goodnight. Lenny
got down under the
blankets. He lay awake for a
long time watching the
shadows moving in the high
roof. He could hear the girls
whispering behind the
curtain, then Winnie began
to cry.

Lenny felt numb. The only
thing that seemed real at
that moment was the
brass badge that Dad had
given him underneath his
pillow. He went to sleep
clutching it.

LENNY woke very early while the girls were still asleep. He could hear faraway stirring noises in the house and faint echoing footsteps, but no one came. He got out of bed, pattered over to the window and pulled the blackout curtain aside.

His mouth fell open.

He looked out over a jumble of roofs and chimneys. Not the squat, blackened kind like they had in London but a fairground of barley-sugar shapes with grinning gargoyle waterspouts winking in the sun. Beyond that, still wrapped in haze, were gardens, outhouses, meadows with great spreading trees and a humped-up hill rising behind like a cut-out paper shape.

So this was the country! He had never seen anything like it.

THE great house which Lenny had come to was very old. It had countless rooms. Lady De Vass, who owned the place, lived in one part, Nanny in another. The army of servants who had once looked after the house and garden had now shrunk down to Mrs B. who cooked, Nelly who helped with the cleaning and washing up, and an old gardener called Bill Penny.

The evacuees had their breakfast in a kitchen as big as the synagogue Lenny went to at home. It was warm in there but Lenny was shy and miserable. Nelly smiled at him.

THERE was porridge with plenty of milk and thick slices of bread and marge. But Mrs B. was cross when Lenny would not eat the bacon she gave him.

'There's good food wasted! I'll not have that!' she scolded. 'We don't eat bacon in our family,' said Lenny in a low voice.

Everyone stopped eating and stared at him. Joyce's eyes were as round and as hard as marbles. Even Winnie stopped grizzling. Lenny felt his ears turning pink. But he was stubborn. He thought of Mum and Dad and he still wouldn't eat the bacon. In the end Mrs B. gave in and told the children to take their dirty plates into the scullery and get out from under her feet.

THE girls went off giggling, trailing Winnie after them. Lenny did not know what he was supposed to do so he wandered off into the yard, through a big gate and into the gardens.

He walked along paths with wide overgrown flowerbeds and peeped into long greenhouses. He found a goldfish pond like the one in the park at home but it was choked with weeds and the fish had gone.

THERE was a summerhouse half hidden in ivy and beyond it, set in a high stone wall, a wooden door.

It was not the door to somebody's house, Lenny knew that. It was a garden door. He remembered hearing somewhere about a secret garden that was locked up for years and years and nobody ever went in.

Cautiously he pushed the door. It creaked open.

INSIDE was a little garden, like a room without a roof. It had criss-cross mossy paths lined with knee-high hedges and stone seats. In the centre was a great rose bush with trailers which swept the ground.

It was very quiet in there. Then a bird flew up with a great clatter of wings and Lenny saw something on the far side of the garden, high up on a pedestal by the wall. At first he thought it was something alive and watching him. But it was too still to be alive. He went over to it.

It was a unicorn, carved in stone, just like the one on his badge. It did not look fierce. Strong, perhaps, and very beautiful, with its curved neck and long mane. Prancing there alone in the shadow of the wall it seemed as lonely as he was.

Lenny felt a huge relief to have found this place. It made him feel more like himself again. He made up his mind to come back there whenever he could.

On Monday morning the evacuees started at the village school. The children were not friendly. They looked at Lenny blankly as though he wasn't there. When the bell went for morning prayers Lenny had to stay alone in the classroom, sitting at a desk.

In the playground Joyce, Patsy and Winnie went off together. Lenny was not included in the boys' football game. He stood by the wall until it was time to go home, clutching Dad's badge in his pocket and pretending he didn't care.

On Saturday nights the evacuees had a bath and Nanny inspected their heads for nits. The bath was huge and had iron feet with claws like a lion. They were only allowed four inches of hot water (it was rationed, like almost everything else) and by the time it was Lenny's turn it wasn't even hot any more.

JOYCE was Nanny's favourite. Nanny curled her hair for her and pressed her hair ribbons for church on Sunday. Joyce put on a special cute voice when she talked to grownups, but when the evacuees were on their own she was sharp-tongued and treacherous.

LENNY spent a lot of time wandering alone in the gardens where no one bothered him. One afternoon when he pushed open the door of the walled garden he found somebody else there. A young man with one leg was sitting on one of the stone benches. He was wearing an old tweed jacket with patched elbows. His empty trouser leg was pinned up and his crutches were propped neatly against the bench beside him.

'Hello there,' said the man. 'It's all right - I do live here. I was just trying to do a bit of weeding.'

'Are you Bill Penny's helper?' Lenny asked him. 'Sort of,' said the man. 'I used to shoot rabbits and pigeons when they got into his vegetable garden but I don't any more. This is one of my favourite places.'

Lenny hovered by the
gate, not sure what to say
next.

'My name's Mick,' the man
continued. 'Don't let me
having one leg bother you.'
'How did you lose it?' Lenny
wanted to know.
'I left it on a beach in
France,' the man told him.
'But I'll be getting a new
one soon.'
'Will it be wooden?'
'No, light metal, I think.
With joints.'

There was a friendly silence.
Then Lenny remembered
he was not to talk to
strangers. He was not sure
whether as this man lived
here he counted as a
stranger or not, but he
thought he had better be
on the safe side.

'I've got to go now,' he said.

Mick just waved.

ON wet days Lenny sometimes followed Nelly about the house and they chatted while she dusted and polished.

In the great hall there was a suit of armour, swords hanging on the walls and pictures of battle scenes with soldiers in red coats. There was one full-length portrait of a very grand officer in splendid uniform.

'That's Lady De Vass's grandfather,' said Nelly. 'They've got a lot of soldiers in the family. Lady De Vass's husband was killed fighting in the First World War and her son's a war hero. He's got medals and all.'

'My dad's in the army,' Lenny told her.
'I'm joining up myself soon,' said Nelly. 'Women's Land Army.'

Lenny longed for Mum to come but she wrote to say that she would not visit 'until he had settled down'. She was working in a fireman's canteen. She was not a good writer and her letters were short. But she saved up her sweet ration and sent Lenny a bar of chocolate now and again.

Lenny saw Mick about the place sometimes, helping Bill Penny or Lady De Vass, but he never came into the kitchen for his meals.

THERE'S something been
killing rabbits in my
vegetable garden,' said Bill
one afternoon when he was
supping up his tea. 'Not
that I mind,' he added, 'I'm
glad of it.'

'A fox?' suggested Mrs B.

'No, it's never a fox. More
like a big cat. It got some
pigeons too.'

'It'll be one of those wild
cats that's living in the barn,'
said Mrs B. 'Very fierce,
they are.'

'Or perhaps a lion escaped
from the zoo,' said Joyce
slyly, looking sideways at
Lenny. 'Lions kill people.
They wait in the dark and
spring out at you and tear
your stomach out.'

THAT night, long after the others had gone to sleep, Lenny lay awake, listening to the night noises outside. Far away in the dark he thought he heard a growling, purring sound, then a shriek of an animal in pain. He got up and peeped through the curtains. Was there something prowling about? A black shadow moving alongside the hedge?

He hurried back into bed and pulled the blankets over his head.

LENNY thought about Mum and Dad a lot, hoping and hoping they were safe. He longed to see them again.

At school things had got a lot worse. The boys had started to shout things at him and make fun of his name.

'Lenny Levi's done a wee-wee!' they jeered. 'Wets his bed, don't he?'

LENNY turned hot with anger and shame. It was true - about the bed. It was only sometimes, and he didn't think anyone at school knew about it. He guessed that Joyce must have told them.

Nanny was grim-faced in the mornings when she had to deal with wet sheets. But Nelly found out and came to Lenny's rescue.

'You can beat this, Lenny,' she told him. 'Everybody does in the end.'
She smuggled some spare bedclothes into the attic so that Lenny could put them on before Nanny came in the morning.

SHE whisked away wet sheets and washed them herself. And she lent Lenny her big alarm clock. Lenny set it twice in the night and it went off with a great clang, but the girls never woke up.

The bedwetting got better. But the boys at school went on teasing.

ONE afternoon Mick came across Lenny sitting hunched on a bench in the walled garden and politely failed to notice his red-rimmed eyes.

'Homesick?' he asked.
At first Lenny was too upset to answer. Then he blurted out all about what the boys at school had said. 'It's not even true any more! Well, hardly at all. But I don't suppose they'll ever stop saying it.'

'I used to wet my bed when I was your age,' Mick told him. 'It was when they sent me away to boarding school.'
'Had you done something wrong?' asked Lenny.

'No, they thought it would do me good,' said Mick. 'My father went there. It was awful. I got teased all the time. Then it started again when I was in hospital after . . .' He looked down at where his leg had been.

'But you were grown up then!' said Lenny, amazed. 'Yes. I cried a lot too. But I got through it somehow. And so will you, or my name's not Mick De Vass!'

There was a long silence. Lenny stared at Mick. 'You're the war hero!' he said at last. 'You've got medals for bravery - Nelly told me!'

'I was frightened all the time in the fighting,' said Mick. 'But I suppose you can't be brave if you're not frightened in the first place. My father was really brave, a fine officer. I am only a private.'

'My dad's a private,' said Lenny proudly. 'He's fighting the Germans, like you did. I've got his badge.'

'I never wanted to fight Germans or anyone else,' Mick told him. 'It's cruelty, bullying and oppression we're fighting against.' Lenny was not quite sure what this meant but he got the general idea.

'I used to come here to this garden to see the unicorn when I was a boy in the school holidays,' said Mick. 'I used to long to be brave and manly and all the things they wanted me to be. But there are different kinds of courage. And I'll tell you one thing. The boys who say those things to you haven't got much. None at all, in fact!'

Later, when he was alone, Lenny thought a lot about what Mick had said. Gradually the bedwetting stopped altogether. Knowing a real war hero who had had the same problem helped. He even forgot about prowling lions.

But then something happened which was much worse.

MUM's weekly letters stopped coming. Every morning Lenny waited anxiously by the gates for the postman to arrive but there was nothing for him. He told nobody how worried he was. But he started to have bad dreams, about searching for Mum, and running and running, and lions leaping out at him and pinning him down with their terrible teeth and claws.

The bedwetting started again. In the end everything was just too terrible to be borne.

ONE night Lenny waited
till the girls were asleep. He
had his suitcase ready
packed. He put his precious
badge in his pocket and
crept downstairs to the back
kitchen. It was difficult to
unbolt the back door without
making a noise but he
managed it, standing on a
chair.

He was running away. He
had to get back to London.

He planned not to go by
the main drive which went
round the front of the house,
in case he was seen. Instead
he would cut through the
gardens, into the orchard,
through a hole in the hedge
and across the field to the
road.

There was a bright moon.
Lenny's sharp shadow
tracked him nimbly along
the silent paths.

I N the vegetable garden he
scampered past raspberry
beds and rows of staked-up
runner beans where anyone,
or anything, could be hiding.

When he reached the
orchard he broke into a run,
weaving from one tree trunk
to another, crouching low
over his suitcase. When he
reached the hedge he
stopped short.

He thought he heard something moving stealthily and carefully through the grass on the other side. He listened. The whole night seemed to be breathing, purring, growling. He was sure something was coming through the hole in the hedge.

Lenny did not stop to find out what it was. He dropped his suitcase and ran.

Now the dark, many-chimneyed shape of the house seemed to be flying swiftly against the moon, too far away to run to now. But he ran all the same, wildly, until he was heaving for breath. Now he was on the path by the summer-house. He saw the door to the walled garden. He pushed it open, fell inside and slammed it shut behind him.

LENNY was crying now, but he felt safe. The garden was completely quiet. The rosebush was frozen in the moonlight. Underneath, in its dense shadow, something glowed softly. It moved gently.

Lenny wasn't frightened. He went towards it. And at that moment he saw the unicorn.

It was alive, glimmering under the rosebush, sitting on its haunches with its one spiralling horn and its long, white, silky mane. It turned its beautiful neck and looked at him.

Lenny knelt down. He laid his head between its hooves with his face in the grass. He was very tired. Almost at once he fell, as though from a great height, into a deep sleep.

HE woke with the sun hot on his neck. It was morning and the unicorn had gone. The statue was in its usual place, watching over the garden.

Lenny got up and looked around. He knew that something had changed inside him. It seemed now that it was his own night fears which had been chasing him. He went out of the garden, closing the door softly behind him, and began to walk back to the house.

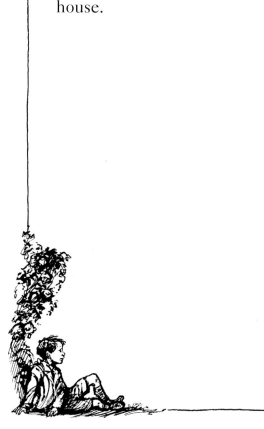

THE lion and the unicorn were back inside Lenny's head; and on his badge. But one important thing was real, and that was what the unicorn stood for.

'Different kinds of courage,' Mick had said. Now, after last night, Lenny thought he really knew what that meant. Perhaps with his new unicorn courage, he would try to stick things out for a bit and see if they got better. Anyway, he didn't seem to care much what Joyce and the rest of them said or did any more. They were only a load of mean, mangy old cats after all.

LENNY came to where
the garden met the back
drive. As he turned the bend
he saw a figure coming
towards the house from the
opposite direction. A smallish
person in a brown coat.
A familiar walk. There was a
good distance between them.
Lenny quickened his pace.
Then he broke into a run.
Now, as he got closer, the
outline of that person was
blurred with tears.

LENNY tore the last few yards. 'Mum - oh Mum!' he shouted. And he threw himself into her arms.

'Didn't you get my letter?' said Mum after a while. 'Bombed out. A direct hit - the whole house gone. Lucky I was working at the canteen that night'.

'I never got no letter', sobbed Lenny. 'The letterbox must have got it,' said Mum. 'I was running away,' Lenny tried to tell her. 'But then...' his voice choked. It was too difficult to explain.

'Lucky you didn't,' said Mum, 'or we might have missed each other. You're a brave boy, Lenny, a proper hero you are. After you left it seemed like even bombs would have been better than us being separated. But now I've come to take you away. We're going to your Auntie Rachel's in Wales. It's by the sea, Lenny. And guess what - your dad's coming home on leave! We'd better go and tell them.'

Lenny felt in his pocket to check that his badge was safe. So he, Lenny Levi, was brave after all. He knew that didn't mean he would never be scared again. But at that moment, he felt he could face anything.

Jaunty now, and hand in hand with Mum, he walked towards the house.